MY FIRST
I Can Read Book®

I See, You Saw

written and illustrated by
Nurit Karlin

HarperCollins*Publishers*

HarperCollins®, 🐾®, and My First I Can Read Book®
are trademarks of HarperCollins Publishers Inc.

Library of Congress Cataloging-in-Publication Data
Karlin, Nurit.
    I see, you saw / by Nurit Karlin.
        p.   cm. — (My first I can read book)
    Summary: Two cats take a stroll and find a seesaw, which one of them saws.
        ISBN 0-06-026677-5. — ISBN 0-06-026678-3 (lib. bdg.)
        [1. Cats—Fiction.]   I. Title.   II. Series.
    PZ7.K1424Iaaj   1997   96-27261
    [E]—dc20   CIP
                                                               AC

2   3   4   5   6   7   8   9   10
❖

I See, You Saw

"Look! A can!"

"I see the can.

"I can kick the can."

"I see a fly.

"I can see the fly fly."

"Look!"

"A seesaw!"

"We can seesaw."

"I see, you saw."

"No. I see, *you* saw.

"I saw the seesaw first!"

"I see a bee."

"I saw the bee."

"I see the sea."

"Look! A saw!"

"I can see the saw."

"I can saw the seesaw."

"Stop! Look up!"

"Where?" "There!"

18

"It is coming down!"

"Quick! Duck!"

Quack

Quack

"It is a duck."

"I see the duck."

"I see a fish."

"I saw the duck fish the fish."

"I saw *you* duck the duck."

"And *I* saw *you*
saw the seesaw."

26480

8/98

$12.89